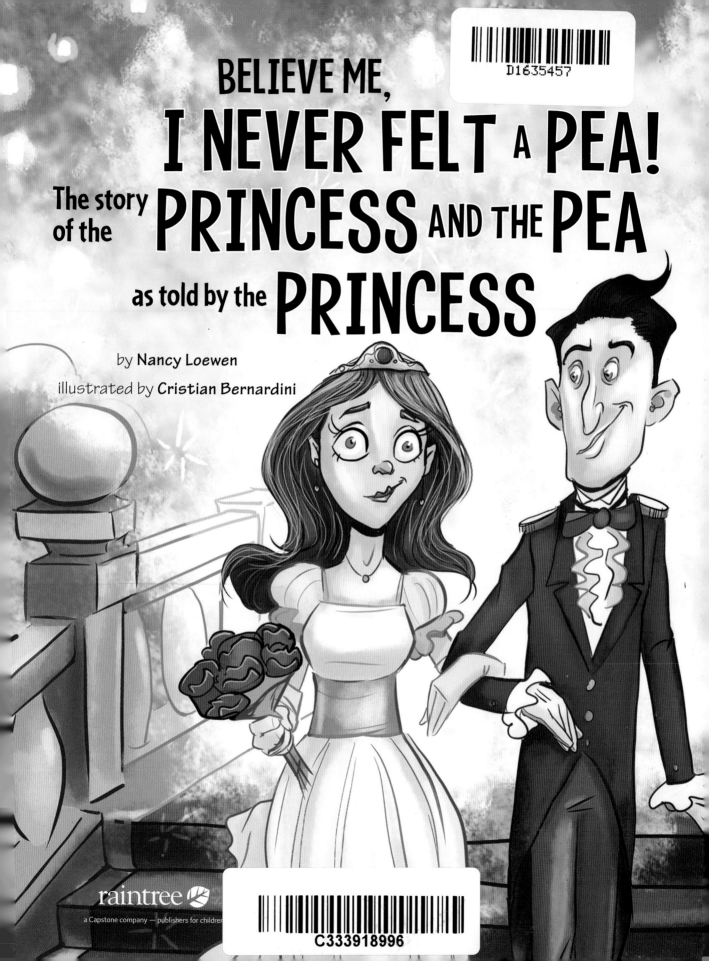

BELIEVE ME, I NEVER FELT A PEA!

The story of the PRINCESS AND THE PEA as told by the PRINCESS

by Nancy Loewen

illustrated by Cristian Bernardini

raintree

a Capstone company — publishers for children

Raintree is an imprint of Capstone Global Library Limited, a company incorporated in England and Wales having its registered office at 7 Pilgrim Street, London, EC4V 6LB – Registered company number: 6695582

www.raintree.co.uk
myorders@raintree.co.uk

Editor: Jill Kalz
Designer: Ted Williams
Creative Director: Nathan Gassman
Production Specialist: Jennifer Walker
The illustrations in this book were created digitally.
Printed and bound in China.

ISBN 978 1 4747 1013 8
20 19 18 17 16
10 9 8 7 6 5 4 3 2 1

British Library Cataloguing in Publication Data
A full catalogue record for this book is available from the British Library.

Special thanks to our adviser, Terry Flaherty, PhD, Professor of English, Minnesota State University, Mankato, USA, for his expertise.

Every effort has been made to contact copyright holders of material reproduced in this book. Any omissions will be rectified in subsequent printings if notice is given to the publisher.

All the internet addresses (URLs) given in this book were valid at the time of going to press. However, due to the dynamic nature of the internet, some addresses may have changed, or sites may have changed or ceased to exist since publication. While the author and publisher regret any inconvenience this may cause readers, no responsibility for any such changes can be accepted by either the author or the publisher.

Can you keep a secret?

I mean a real lips-sealed-and-throw-away-the-key secret.

You can? OK, good. Here goes.

I'm not a real princess.

SHHHH!

Yes, I slept on a pile of 20 mattresses. Yes, it was the worst night's sleep I'd ever had. And yes, I did marry Prince Matthew.

But there's a lot more to the story than that...

The first thing you should know is that Prince Matthew (Matt) wasn't all that interested in getting married. His dream? To be a successful businessman. He came up with one crazy idea after another:

Grape Plate
Berry Medley
Plum
Prune Surprise
Purple Cabbage
Casserole

turning the royal castle into a **hotel**...

opening a **restaurant** that served only purple food...

creating **self-cleaning** horse-drawn carriages...

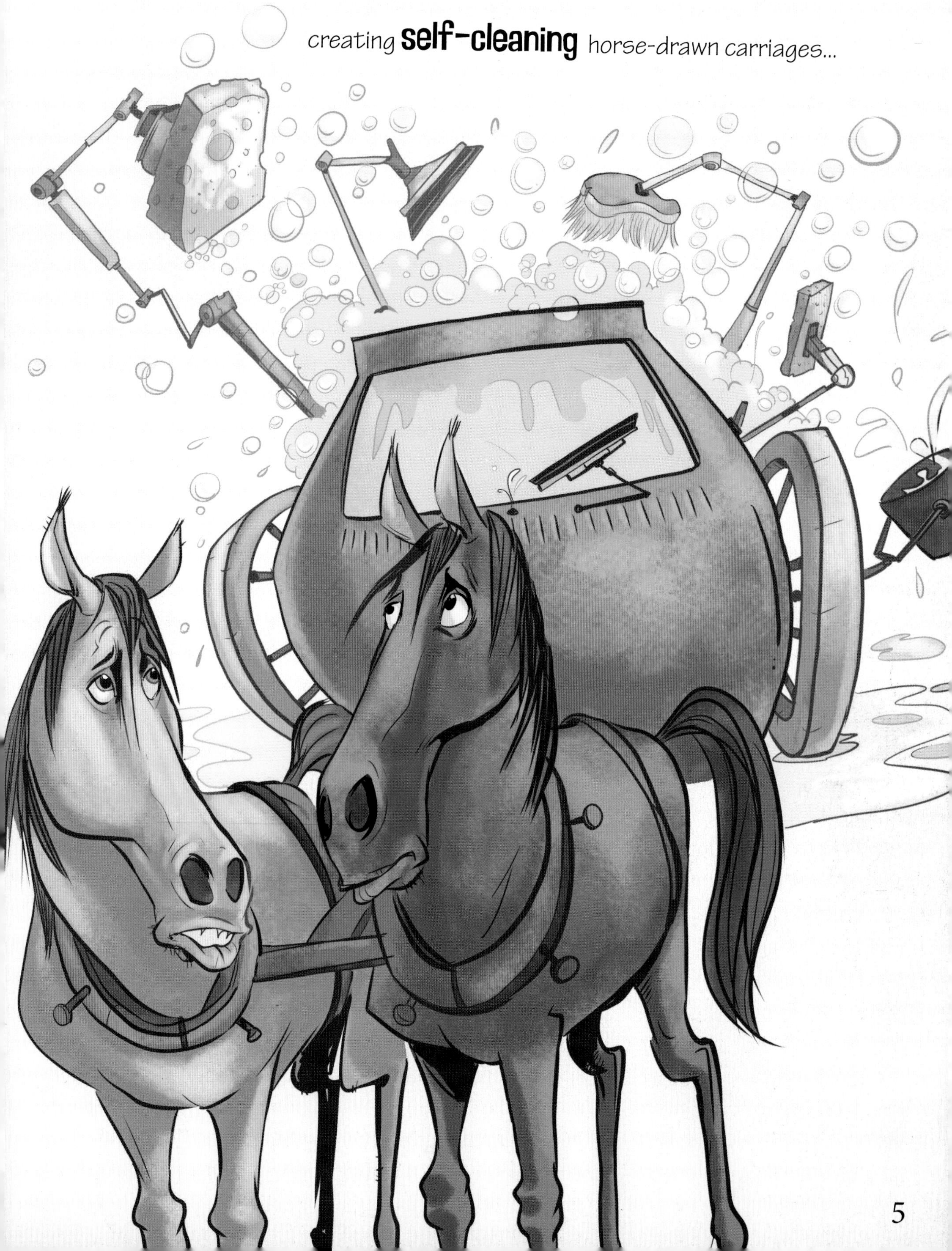

But the queen didn't want her son to go into business. She thought if he was married to a spoiled, pampered girl – a "real princess", in other words – he wouldn't have time for his silly dreams.

She travelled all over the land, testing princesses to make sure they were the real thing. But none met with her approval.

One princess politely ate tough steak rather than demanding a tender piece. **FAIL.**

Another princess carried her own luggage. **FAIL.**

Several princesses wore the same gown two days in a row. **FAIL.**

This is where I come in. And my dog. His name is Prince Super-Pooch, or Prince S for short. Isn't that cute?

One night Prince S and I went for a walk in the woods. Suddenly – **CRACK! BOOM! FLASH!** – a storm came up. We needed shelter, and I knew the castle was near by. I picked up Prince S and made a run for it.

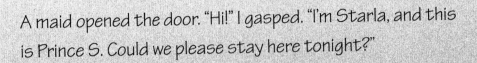

A maid opened the door. "Hi!" I gasped. "I'm Starla, and this is Prince S. Could we please stay here tonight?"

"Ah. Another princess," the maid muttered in an unfriendly way. "Follow me."

"No, I'm not a princess – Prince S is the name of my DOG," I tried to explain, but she didn't pay any attention. Perhaps she couldn't hear me because of the thunder.

The maid showed me to a bedroom, and my jaw dropped. There stood a towering pile of mattresses.

"Excuse me," I said, "but I don't need anything so grand. Really, just throw a sleeping bag on the floor and I'll be fine!"

The maid sniffed rudely and left.

I carefully counted the mattresses – **20 in all!**
Prince S pawed at the bottom mattress, like he does
when there's a crumb under the cupboard he can't reach.

"Stop that," I said. "We're guests here. Be good."

The bed was extremely soft and very comfortable. The
sheets were as smooth as silk and smelled like a flower
garden. I soon fell asleep.

But not for long.

I must have rolled over a little too far, because the next thing I knew – **THWACK!** I hit the floor. Hard. Beds like that should come with guard rails. Or even parachutes.

I climbed back up the ladder and spent the rest of the night staring at the ceiling. I was too scared to move.

The next morning I was tired and grumpy. "I hardly slept a wink!" I said. "Do you see these bruises? I can't wait to go home and sleep in a normal bed."

The maid stared at me for a moment. Then her face lit up. **"Your Majesty! Your Majesty!"** she shouted as she ran down the corridor. "This girl IS a real princess! She complained about the pea!"

So THAT'S what Prince S was trying to get at beneath all those mattresses. A pea! That ridiculous bed was a test.

"Again, Prince S is the name of my DOG!" I called after her. **"I didn't say anything about a pea!"**

But you know how fairy-tale weddings go. There's no stopping them. Beautiful gowns appear, the castle glitters and gleams, music fills the air, crowds gather...

And suddenly there I was.

Married.

To a prince!

Luckily Matt and I love each other. And married life hasn't caused him to give up his dreams. In fact, we're business partners. We've been very successful – **selling mattresses!**

Say YES to the best—a PRINCESS MATTRESS!

Have a ROYAL night's rest on a PRINCESS MATTRESS!

SALE

Discussion points

Look in your local library or online for a copy of "The Princess and the Pea", the original version by Hans Christian Andersen. Explain how the original story and the version you have just read are alike. Explain how they are different.

How do the maid's actions affect the plot of this story?

Describe Prince Matthew. What information about him comes from Starla? What information comes from the illustrations?

This story is told from Starla's point of view. If the maid told the story, what details might she tell differently? What if the queen told the story? How would her point of view differ?

Glossary

character person, animal or creature in a story
plot what happens in a story
point of view way of looking at something
version account of something from a certain point of view

Read more

Hans Christian Andersen's Fairy Tales (Usborne Illustrated), retold by Anna Milbourne, Gillian Doherty & Ruth Brocklehurst (Usborne Publishing Ltd, 2012)

The Poodle and the Pea (Animal Fairy Tales), Charlotte Guillain (Raintree, 2013)

The Princess and the Pea, Lauren Child (Puffin, 2006)

Sleeping Handsome and the Princess Engineer (Fairy Tales Today), Kay Woodward (Curious Fox, 2015)

Website

www.bbc.co.uk/cbeebies/stories/melody-princess-and-the-pea

Listen to the story of a prince who wants to find a real princess.

Look out for all the books in this series:

Believe Me, Goldilocks Rocks!
Believe Me, I Never Felt a Pea!
Frankly, I'd Rather Spin Myself a New Name!
Frankly, I Never Wanted to Kiss Anybody!
Honestly, Red Riding Hood Was Rotten!
No Kidding, Mermaids Are a Joke!
No Lie, I Acted Like a Beast!

No Lie, Pigs (and Their Houses) CAN Fly!
Really, Rapunzel Needed a Haircut!
Seriously, Cinderella Is SO Annoying!
Seriously, Snow White Was SO Forgetful!
Truly, We Both Loved Beauty Dearly!
Trust Me, Hansel and Gretel Are SWEET!
Trust Me, Jack's Beanstalk Stinks!